A Pocket Full of Kisses

Audrey Penn

Illustrated by Barbara Leonard Gibson

Child & Family Press • Washington, DC

CHILD WELFARE LEAGUE OF AMERICA, INC.
HEADQUARTERS
440 First Street, NW, Third Floor,
Washington, DC 20001-2085
E-mail: books@cwla.org

CURRENT PRINTING (last digit)
10 9 8 7 6 5 4 3 2 1
Printed in the United States of America

Text design by James Melvin
Edited by Tegan A. Culler

ISBN # 0-87868-894-3

Library of Congress Cataloging-in-Publication Data

Penn, Audrey, 1947-
  A pocket full of kisses / by Audrey Penn ; illustrated by Barbara Leonard Gibson.
      p. cm.
  Summary: Chester Raccoon is worried that his mother does not have enough love for both him and his new baby brother.
  ISBN 0-87868-894-3 (hardcover : alk. paper)
  [1. Mother and child--Fiction. 2. Love--Fiction. 3. Babies--Fiction. 4. Raccoons--Fiction.] I. Gibson, Barbara, ill. II. Title.

  PZ7.P38448Po 2004
  [E]--dc22

2004006046

For my darlings,
Matthew, Ryan, Daniella, and Rebecca
–AP

For my father
and his grandchildren,
Caitlin and Evan
–BLG

Chester Raccoon sat in the hollow of a tree stump and pouted. "Please, can we give him back?" he asked his mother. "I'll be really, *really* good if we can give him back."

Mrs. Raccoon smiled tenderly. "You're already really, really good, Chester. But I'm afraid no matter how good you are, we can't give him back. Besides, I thought you liked having a little brother."

"I did like it, at first," admitted Chester. "But now he plays with my toys, and swings on my swings, and reads my books. Then he pulls my tail and talks to my friends and follows me everywhere I go!"

Mrs. Raccoon lifted Chester onto her lap and smoothed out his worried, furry forehead. "That's what little brothers do," she explained in a very motherly tone. "It's no different than sharing the woods, or sharing the stream, or sharing the food we find. Ronny wants to be just like you."

Mrs. Raccoon placed Chester on the ground and smiled at him with the soft, loving eyes he knew so well. "I think someone needs a Kissing Hand," she said, in a voice that was warm and inviting. She took Chester's hand in her own and spread open his tiny fingers into a fan. Leaning over, she kissed him right in the middle of his palm.

Chester felt the warmth of that kiss rush from his hand, up his arm, and into his heart. And when he pressed his hand to his cheek, he could hear his mother's words in his head. "Mommy loves you," they said. "Mommy loves you."

Chester grinned so wide, the tips of his silky black mask crinkled upward. Even his cheeks flushed to a primrose pink. He was the happiest raccoon in the forest.

Then, in the blink of a moment, all the joy went out of the little raccoon. His pink cheeks paled, and a stream of tiny, hot tears fell like spring rain down his sad little face.

Even his silky black mask drooped as he watched his mother reach down, take Ronny's hand in her own, open his tiny fingers into a fan, and kiss his brother right in the middle of his palm.

"That was *my* Kissing Hand," Chester gasped
in the saddest voice his mother had ever heard.
"Why did you give Ronny *my* Kissing Hand?
Don't you love me anymore?"

"Oh, Chester!" cried Mrs. Raccoon. "Of course I love you!"

"Then how come you gave the baby *my* Kissing Hand?" asked Chester.

Mrs. Raccoon gathered Chester up in her arms and gave him a great, big, comforting hug. "I would never give Ronny your Kissing Hand," she assured him gently. "That was *his* Kissing Hand. Now you each have one of your own."

Chester wiped away his tears and settled in his mother's lap. "If you give both of us Kissing Hands, won't you run out?"

Mrs. Raccoon laughed. "Would you like to hear a story?" she asked Chester.

"About kisses?"

"About stars," said Mrs. Raccoon.

"Every night, just before the sun goes down, it reaches out with its rays and touches every star in the universe. One by one, the stars light up and shine down upon us. Even on nights we can't see the stars, they're up there sparkling away. No matter how many stars fill the sky, the sun will never run out of light, and its rays will never stop reaching out to them.

"That's the way it is with Kissing Hands. When somebody loves you, their kisses are like the sun's rays—always there and always shining. No matter how many Kissing Hands I give you and Ronny, I will never, *ever* run out."

"But you are right about one thing," Mrs. Raccoon told Chester.

Ronny's big brother widened his eyes and looked surprised. "What's that?" he asked his mother.

"You are the big brother, and that deserves something extra special."

Mrs. Raccoon put Ronny on a swing, then took Chester's right hand in hers and spread open his tiny fingers into a fan. Leaning over, she kissed him right in the middle of his palm.

"That kiss is for your pocket," she told him.
"Take good care of it, and keep it as a spare.
You never know when a big brother might
need a little extra care."

Chester hugged his mother and romped
away. "I love you, too," he seemed to say.